Dear Parents and Educators,

Welcome to Penguin Young Readers! As parents and educators, you know that each child develops at his or her own pace—in terms of speech, critical thinking, and, of course, reading. Penguin Young Readers recognizes this fact. As a result, each Penguin Young Readers book is assigned a traditional easy-to-read level (1–4) as well as a Guided Reading Level (A–P). Both of these systems will help you choose the right book for your child. Please refer to the back of each book for specific leveling information. Penguin Young Readers features esteemed authors and illustrators, stories about favorite characters, fascinating nonfiction, and more!

Vroom, Zoom, Bud

LEVEL **1**

GUIDED READING LEVEL **D**

This book is perfect for an **Emergent Reader** who:
- can read in a left-to-right and top-to-bottom progression;
- can recognize some beginning and ending letter sounds;
- can use picture clues to help tell the story; and
- can understand the basic plot and sequence of simple stories.

Here are some **activities** you can do during and after reading this book:
- Make Connections: In this story, Bud wants to race, but he also wants to play in a mud puddle. Have you ever wanted to do two things at the same time? How did it make you feel? What did you do?
- Rhyming Words: On a separate piece of paper, make a list of all the rhyming words in this story. For example, *Bud* rhymes with *mud* so write those two words next to each other.

Remember, sharing the love of reading with a child is the best gift you can give!

—Bonnie Bader, EdM
 Penguin Young Readers program

*Penguin Young Readers are leveled by independent reviewers applying the standards developed by Irene Fountas and Gay Su Pinnell in *Matching Books to Readers: Using Leveled Books in Guided Reading*, Heinemann, 1999.

For Fiona Kenshole: This is for you, with my
enormous thanks—PL

To Jessika, for always getting me outside to
play in the mud—CA

PENGUIN YOUNG READERS
An Imprint of Penguin Random House LLC

Penguin supports copyright. Copyright fuels creativity, encourages diverse voices, promotes free
speech, and creates a vibrant culture. Thank you for buying an authorized edition of this book and for
complying with copyright laws by not reproducing, scanning, or distributing any part of it in any form
without permission. You are supporting writers and allowing Penguin to continue to publish books
for every reader.

Text copyright © 2016 by Patricia Lakin. Illustrations copyright © 2016 by Penguin Random House LLC.
All rights reserved. Published by Penguin Young Readers, an imprint of Penguin Random House LLC,
345 Hudson Street, New York, New York 10014. Manufactured in China.

Library of Congress Cataloging-in-Publication Data is available.

ISBN 978-0-448-48832-5 (pbk)   10 9 8 7 6 5 4 3 2 1
ISBN 978-0-448-48833-2 (hc)   10 9 8 7 6 5 4 3 2

Vroom, Zoom, Bud

by Patricia Lakin
illustrated by Cale Atkinson

Penguin Young Readers
An Imprint of Penguin Random House

Cars. Cars. Cars.

They zoom this way.

Look! There is a race today!

I like to go fast, too.

I want to race with you.

I run!

I spin!

10

11

I jump high, too.

I want to race with you.

15

Ready! Set!

One! Two! Three!

Is that mud I see?

Muddy, Mud, Bud!

That is me!

21

The race! The race!

It is not done.

I want to win.

I vroom, zoom, run!

Help! Help! Help!

I cannot see.

Have I won?

It was not me!

But I had fun.

I vroomed.

I zoomed.

I went fast.

31

And someone had

to come in last.